LOOP HOLES

Spineless Wonders

ABN 98156041888
PO Box 220
Strawberry Hills, New South Wales
Australia 2012

www.shortaustralianstories.com.au

First published by Spineless Wonders 2016
Text © Susan McCreery

Edited by Bronwyn Mehan and Annie Parkinson. With help from Laura Barry and publishing assistant Nicole Schalchlin.

Illustrations, cover and book design by Bettina Kaiser

All rights reserved. Without limiting the rights under copyright reserved above, no part of this publication may be reproduced, stored in or introduced into a retrieval system, or transmitted in any form or by any means (electronic, mechanical, photocopying, recording or otherwise) without the prior written permission of the publisher of this book.

Typeset in Garamond 11/14

Printed and bound by Lightning Source Australia

National Library of Australia Cataloguing-in-Publication entry

Loopholes/McCreery, Susan
1st ed.

ISBN: 978-1-925052-29-9 (pbk)
ISBN: 978-1-925052-30-5 (ebk)
A823.4

Contents

Biographies	vii
Foreword	x
Breakdown	3
Monoculus	5
Mother's Day	7
Moth Holes	8
106 Hours	11
Missing	13
Spathiphyllum	15
Pet Hate	17
constraint	19
Loose Ends	21
Onion Man	23
Safekeeping	25
Disturbance	27
Rear Window	29
Something You're Not	31
Moored	32
Mexican Stand-off	35
'Tis the Season	37
Subsurface	39
Account	41
Feed the Man	43
'Well, then'	44
Between Dark and Dawn	46
Welcome Party	49
Cooks' War	50
Deterioration	53
Vent	55
Take Us to People	56
Frost	59
Fact or Fiction?	61
Fracking	63
Broken down	65

esc	67	Plumbing	103
Booster	69	Hold-up	105
Drought	71	What He Needs	107
Exhibition	73	Rats	109
Inheritance	75	First Quarter	111
Whimbrel	77	Broken Windows	113
Narcissus	79	Anchor	115
Loadbearing	81	Grand Designs	117
Hardware	82	Flat Pact	119
Manifesto for a Woman Walker	85	Burden	121
outlet	87	The Present	123
Retreat	89	Platitudes	125
Illusion	91	Catch-up	127
Values	93	First Love	129
Mona Lisa	94	Misguided	131
Tough Love	97	Lights	133
Rescued	99	How Do We Do This?	135
We Should So Try That	101	Acknowledgements	137

This project has been assisted by the Australian Government through the Australia Council, its arts funding and advisory body.

Australian Government

Biographies

SUSAN MCCREERY is a writer from Thirroul, NSW. Her microfiction has been published by Spineless Wonders (*Writing to the Edge*, *Flashing the Square*, *Out of Place*), as well as by *Seizure* and *Cuttlefish*. Her poetry and short fiction have appeared in *Best Australian Poems 2009*, *Sleepers Almanac*, *Going Down Swinging*, *Hecate*, *Five Bells*, *Island*, *Award Winning Australian Writing*, *Lost Boy*, *Escape*, *The Trouble with Flying* and *Shibboleth*, among others. Story competition shortlistings include the Overland/Victoria University, the Hal Porter, *The Age*, the Margaret River and the Albury City; prizes include the joanne burns/Flashing the Square, the Carmel Bird, the Bundaberg Writers, the Peter Cowan Writers, and the Julie Lewis. Her poetry collection, *Waiting for the Southerly*, was commended in the Anne Elder award (2012). In 2014 she was awarded a Varuna fellowship and an Australia Society of Authors mentorship for her short story collection. She has worked as professional proofreader for the past eighteen years, and when not at her desk can be found swimming long distances in the ocean.

BETTINA KAISER is a visual artist as well as a graphic and web designer. Bettina has undertaken artistic residencies in Antarctica, at Yvonne and Arthur Boyd's Bundanon and in Milparinka in outback Australia. She won the 2005 Fisher's Ghost Art Award, Contemporary category and has exhibited throughout Australia as well as overseas. Some of her work can be seen on www.bettinakaiser.com

Everything in it is both head and tail.

Charles Baudelaire, *Paris Spleen*

Foreword

I was first drawn to Susan McCreery's work a few years ago when I read her microfiction 'Hold-up' in *Flashing the Square*. Check it out – it's included in this collection and it's amazing. In the space of 172 words, she nails it. She gives us the parameters of a story and trusts us to imagine all the ways it might play out. Her use of implication is nothing short of genius. She doesn't tell us the man is holding a gun, nor that he's threatening the attendant behind the register – but the reader has no doubt both of these things are occurring because of those lifted palms.

But it's not just the action that drives these stories. The intimate details and close observations force McCreery's readers to empathise with her characters – even characters whose moral compass may be skewed. That's why she's such a strong writer – we're compelled to keep reading until the end and when we stop reading we're compelled to keep thinking about the worlds she's shown us.

Here, lucky for us, we get a whole book dedicated to her work. These pieces defy categorisation. Some of them might fit under the term microfiction, while others sway towards the prose poem. McCreery's work spans the continuum between the two, but all of the pieces here invite the reader into worlds much larger than word counts suggest. We see this in 'Hold-up' but it's deftly shown to us again and again throughout *Loopholes*. Read 'Lights', where we're given worlds of character in the minutes while a husband and wife wait at a set of traffic lights. McCreery's use of tone and the way she spins in plot after the fact is masterful. But don't stop there. Marvel at the tight dialogue in 'Drought'. Appreciate the thermos that holds hot comfort in 'Frost'. And by God, check out her verbs. They are full of purpose. And by all means, you should join the verb debate in 'Mother's Day'.

As an immigrant to Australia, one of the things I appreciate through all of these stories is how this country – the land, the culture – reverberates through the text. Thank you to McCreery for capturing this complex and multi-faceted place and thank you to Spineless Wonders for ensuring that effort can be appreciated. This is a collection that is meant to be savoured – count yourself lucky. You're at the beginning. You have all of these story-poems to look forward to.

~ Shady Cosgrove, 2016

Breakdown

The young couple headed west where no one knew them. They sang with the windows down and touched each other's thighs. The horizon stretched forever. Several hours in, the engine began to make knocking noises, so they pulled over at a viewing platform. The girl lifted the bonnet. The radiator was hot so she asked her boyfriend to take off his t-shirt. She held it over the cap and twisted. At the sudden hiss of steam she jumped back, banging her head. When her boyfriend laughed, she swore at him and stormed off across the plain. He yelled after her, saying they should have had the car checked over before they left. He'd told her that.

Before long a bus could be seen in the distance. The couple, who'd been wordless for a time, watched as passengers, bewildered by the heat and glare, stepped down. Some hung back from the platform, nervous about the height. They shaded their eyes, sipped at water bottles, took photos of the ribbony road.

A man with a baby on his hip strolled over to the couple's car. The baby wore a white cotton hat with a lace trim. Its pudgy legs kicked. Its cheeks were aflame. The man fiddled under the bonnet for a few moments. *That should get you to the roadhouse*, he said. *But they won't fix it for you. After that*, he swept his arm from horizon to horizon as the baby gave a gummy laugh, *after that, you're on your own.*

Monoculus

He held his new glass eye up to the light. I like it, he said. It has boldness. Depth.

He fitted the eye and set its gaze on her, penetrating, unwavering.

She said, Don't look at me like that.

I can't help it, he said. It's the eye. It has boldness, depth. I can't change its expression.

Then buy another one, she said. I can't stand being looked at like that all day.

It was the last one in the shipment, he said. I'd have to wait three months for another selection. They're not easy to obtain.

I can wait three months if it means I get an eye that looks at me tenderly. Can't you order a tender eye?

I don't think they make tender eyes.

Well, what *are* the options?

Bold. Cruel. Distant. Unfathomable.

Can't say I like any of them. How about you just take it out and we live with empty for a while? Empty. Yes. That could work.

Mother's Day

Driving south, to the supermarket, I see a makeshift placard on the side of the road.

FLOWER

Noun or verb?

The choice is breaking me.

Moth Holes

Remember Istanbul? she asked.

Oh, yes, he said. I do. Topkapi Palace. The Harem. The emerald dagger. The Blue Mosque.

Not so much the attractions. What happened.

It Happened in Istanbul. Sounds like a movie.

Well, do you remember?

Prompt, please.

We were in the bazaar – you were haggling over a rug. I was in another shop trying on this green suede jacket.

Did I buy the rug?

You're standing on it!

He looked down. Nice rug. I like the little houses.

I think they're mosques. See the minarets?

Could be.

Anyway, the owner – the shop with the green jacket – he was a sleaze. But I wanted that jacket.

What did he do?

You don't remember? Stuck his tongue in my ear.

You should have walked out, darling.

At the time you thought it was hilarious. And you know what? I've never worn it. Not once. So, I've been thinking about this lately. The fact that I allowed him to do that, and I bought his jacket. He was the winner – twice over. Must have thought I was a prime female tourist idiot.

He shook his head. Why is this an issue now? It's twenty years ago.

Moth holes.

In what? The jacket?

She held up the jacket, looked at it thoughtfully. Mmm. Among other things.

106 Hours

I'm seated at a table in the square trying not to write the same anecdotes and travel insights on four different postcards. I'd hate to be found out repeating 'the light here is extraordinary' or 'I've finally figured out how to ask for a beer!!!☺'. Who sends postcards anymore? The recipients will appreciate the gesture because they're either very old, or very into handmade and vegetables, or they're my partner. I flex my fingers and look around. The light really *is* extraordinary. It shimmers off doorways and pots of geraniums and olive oil bottles. I sip my beer. The last postcard is the trickiest, because I need to find a considerate way of saying I'm not coming back. As I'm thinking about this, my phone pings with a message: 'Miss u love u only 106 more hours'. I put down my glass and thumb out a reply: 'Can't wait wish u were here.'

Missing

Amy could still hear them gabbing away, arguing about which track to take. Once her eyes had adjusted she saw that the cave was in fact a tunnel and a sharp thrill coursed through her at the prospect of exploring on her own. No one would miss her. Least of all her dad, who was always so wrapped up in Laura. He and Josh were yelling at each other. It's *that* way. No, it's downhill, you idiot. It's *that* way. Josh stood up for himself these days, now that he was sixteen. Amy didn't have the nerve to argue with her dad. Stupid Laura was giggling her annoying high-pitched giggle. She hadn't even wanted to go on a bushwalk, you could tell that a mile off. Not her 'thing' and anyway she always wanted Amy's dad to herself. Amy hated all the changes since Laura had moved in. Bossing them around, telling them to tidy up, put things away, make their beds. Her dad never said a word. *Amy!* That was Laura. *Finally* they noticed she was missing. Shut up, Laura. You're not my mother. *Amy!* That was her dad, following Laura's lead as usual. The cave-tunnel wasn't scary at all. It was cosy. No one could get to her, tell her what to do. *Amy!* That was her brother now. Josh, who was hardly ever at home. They used to be a team. *Amy!* Josh sounded worried, just like the old Josh. For this Josh she might come out. Might.

Spathiphyllum

A draught can chill you. I have to keep you lightly warm. You watch me, turning your spaghetti neck when I'm not looking. White sail! Lily of peace! I'm not fooled by your self-containment. You're not so resilient. When I forget you, you bow low. Your glossy frill dims without me. Your tips can burn. What if I raised the blind? Let the sun at you? You'd need me then. You'd beg for me then. It's inevitable – your spadix will go green with age.

Pet Hate

A man owned a shop selling peanuts to monkeys. The monkeys would line up in a disorderly fashion, brown paper bags at the ready. One morning a dog stopped by and said, Wish there was a shop selling ham bones. Why isn't someone selling bones to dogs? The monkeys nodded in agreement. The man had a brother who was looking for a useful job, so he took over the lease of the neighbouring shop and before long dogs were lining up for ham bones. The cats got wind of it and complained there was nothing for them. A shop selling sardines would be ace. Before long the entire strip was devoted to servicing the animals of the area. The humans began to see red. Since when are our pets on the top rung? they cried. What happened to *our* needs? And they pulled at their chains and howled from their kennels and dug holes in frustration. The animals yelled at them to shut up. One old dog gave a human a sharp kick in the ribs.

constraint

early days of spring warmth, girl 11? 12? shorts, sandals, crop-top, dog on lead, waits to cross at lights, ice-cream? bread? milk? thin-strapped purse, gift? purchase? boy 11? 12? skate shoes, cap, loose t-shirt, skateboard, new? hand-me-down? waits to cross at lights, mates? park? fun? girl tugs down top, touches hair, lowers head, pulls bag tight, lights change *Walk*, boy slaps skateboard to bitumen, girl moves straight, boy diagonal, girl steps up kerb, secures dog to pole, boy leaps up kerb, swerves to avoid, sails away, gone

Loose Ends

Not a pretty sight, his feet, thought Alan. Pale toes bristling with ginger hairs. Nails in need of a clip. His coffee arrived a few seconds later. Alan couldn't quite believe the luxury of sitting in a café on a Thursday morning. It was all thanks to China. Cheap manufacturing. He'd never been to China. Never been anywhere. His feet were starting to take on a mauve tinge. Too early in the season to be wearing thongs – Judith could have told him that. 'You need a jacket,' she'd say. Uncanny ability. Always a brolly on hand if it rained. Like a bird about weather was Judith – the way they cut the cackle before a storm. Or carry on like a circus on a warm bright morning. 'Just a t-shirt, I reckon, love. And a cap.' The spoon was clean, shiny. The coffee at work used to stick to the teaspoons like gobs of brown cement. He missed the staffroom. Fifteen years. Alan looked out the window at the passers-by. How many of them were out of work? What would he do for the rest of the day?

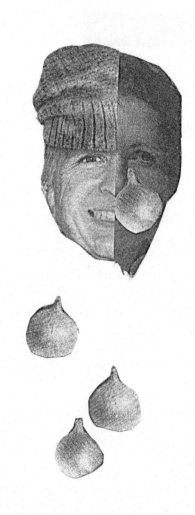

Onion Man

He was a great believer in onions. Cut them up and lay them raw round the house to suck up cold viruses. *He must have cried a lot.* I nodded. Yes! Always streaming snot and tears. We bought cartons of tissues. *Worse than a cold, I would have thought.* Yes! There's no other way to put it. Onion man was a bit of a knob. Anyhow, he finally lands a job, and of course – onions *verboten* in the office. So – get this – within two days he has a sore throat. He's back home cutting up onions. This cycle continued for a year. *You should call it 'My Year of the Onion'.* Yes! I was so glad when he peeled off, taking his sulphites with him. Ever since, the mere mention of onion brings me to tears.

Safekeeping

On the way back from hospital the day my mother collapsed, I bought some leather-revitalising wax. Her handbag, which I'd taken for safekeeping despite the nurse's arched brow, was a shabby navy, the strap shot with hairline cracks.

Armed with a strip of old singlet from her cleaning cupboard, I sat down to empty it at her kitchen table. Out tumbled a coin purse, a wad of receipts bound in elastic, and a breath-freshener. In the pockets I found notepaper, a loyalty card, bent safety pins, a couple of loose pellets of gum, and a flaky headache tablet in a blister square. One by one I unrolled the receipts. All liquor outlets of various locations, some across town. Since my mouth was open, I sprayed it with spearmint and nearly choked.

I shook the bag free of grit, then proceeded to work the wax into the worn hide. Before long, it began to gleam and soften under my fingertips.

When I'd finished, I disposed of the tablet and gum and replaced the other items. I zipped the bag, then held it at arm's length, admiring, before pressing it to my face.

Disturbance

Crash. The newlyweds were at it again. Moved in three months ago and barely a night without a fight. You'd never know it to look at them. Arms twined round each other in the lift, sweet as sweet. He holds her really tight. She's shedding that weight, too – just as she should, being a fitness instructor. What a racket. He cranked up the volume on the TV – Danish crime drama, so the sound wasn't important, but he liked the lilt of the dialogue. *Thud.* Who would be married? Thank Christ he was single again. Once bitten. He and Shalema used to fight. She pulled an AVO on him. Where'd she get the idea he wanted to hurt her? Oh, waa-waa, so he twisted her arm. Once. Could hardly see the mark after a week. Nothing broken. Spitting at her? Spitting's not punching. And the time her head collided with his fist, well she carried on as though it was deliberate. *Slam.* That was their door. Silence. Thank Christ. She's probably running away. They all do that. But they're so easy to track down. *So* easy.

Rear Window

He wore a suit well, she thought, despite his bulk. She left him where he lay on the floor and took her martini to the window seat. Time enough to dispose of the body. All she'd need was a stout suitcase or two. She sucked the olive off the swizzle stick and chuckled at the idea: *Ding-Dong. Avon calling!* Heck, that dancer was at her practice again, thump-thump-thump. She inclined an ankle this way and that, admiring her new slingbacks. How peaceful it was in the apartment without his incessant carping and his dark moods. She certainly felt a whole lot better. The woman on the balcony above was reeling in her yappy dog in its ridiculous little basket. Her eyes moved up to the apartment across the courtyard. Heck, there he was at the window – the photographer with the broken leg and fashion-plate girlfriend and nothing better to do than spy on his neighbours. She switched off the lamp and lit a cigarette. When would this heat break?

Something You're Not

The tent fabric whipped in the wet wind. Jason's sleeping bag, thin as it was, offered no comfort. He squirrelled down to warm it with his breath. His tent-mate, Jack, was whimpering ever so slightly, barely audible. The two were not close friends, but here, this night, they were.

You cold? ventured Jason, from deep within his sleeping bag.

Mmm, said Jack, teeth chattering. It's awful. I can't sleep. I hate Scouts.

Me too. I never wanted to join. What's the point of knots?

The wind picked up and began to howl.

I'm going to quit, said Jason, his head back in the open. I don't care what he says.

He? said Jack. Your dad?

Stepdad. He always tells me Scouts made him into the man he is.

My mum says I have to do it because it teaches values. And it's good for *boys*.

After a moment Jason said, The whole thing sucks. I don't see why I should have to lie here freezing my nuts off. Just so I can become a man like *him*.

Moored

You remember this one? he said. The Owl and the Pussycat?

No, no I don't, she said.

What? Never heard of the pea-green boat? *Oh lovely pussy—*

She gave him a shove.

What was that for? Then he understood. It's a *cat*. The owl is singing about a cat. It's a love song. *What a beautiful pussy(cat) you are.* See? No call for violence. It's a love song.

When did pussy come to mean ... you know?

Long afterwards, I guess.

I liked *pea-green boat*.

Let's sail away! he exclaimed. For a year and a day. Let's do it.

Where to?

We could go to the land where the bong-tree grows. And dance by the light of the—

Ah, the *bong*-tree. That old territory, huh?

He trailed off then, tired. There would be no boat, no pussy, no dancing.

They would go for a drink at the pub and he would complain about his boss. They'd be home in time for the footy and he'd have a beer and she'd get annoyed and ring her mother and then they'd go to bed.

Mexican Stand-off

A man leaves his son in the desert, saying, 'Here, you will become a man.' He returns in ten days to find nothing but rotting flesh. He kneels to weep, 'What have I done?' before heading home to his wife, who cries, 'Where is my son? You too must go into the desert to become a man.' She drives to the road's end. Thrusts her husband into the searing sun. For days he digs for food, finding none. A scorpion appears. Man and arthropod circle each other, threatening, waiting.

'Tis the Season

Dale dragged the box of Christmas lights off the listing metal storage unit and began the annual task of disentanglement. Within five minutes he was fed up and instead started to rearrange the remaining boxes, wondering if he could be bothered to colour-code. Wait, this was an odd one. He opened it, peered in to find Marnie's Travels Without My Husband memorabilia, courtesy their time in counselling. Loose and unwound in Italy, Morocco, Peru, sampling exotic food, beds. Dale released a tiny puff of scorn.

Since he was in the garage it wasn't much of a stretch to reach across to the shadow-shape wall, take the shears, and, mirroring his movements for clipping the box hedge around her souvenir fake marble Venus, snip (with little regard for shape) the bundle of tangled wires and tiny fragile bulbs – chop, chop, chop.

Account

The government needs to do more. Life jackets should be just like seatbelts. Peel spuds. The third inquest. An earlier breakdown. Both lanes stretching from the M4. An extra sixty- to ninety-minute travel time. Boil water. Know the dangers. Drivers battle fatigue and race to meet deadlines. Finger of blame aimed squarely at the big supermarket chains. Gorilla on. Faulty indicators. Unsecured loads. A senate inquiry. Rogue drivers. The top of the chain to be held accountable. Plastic chops. Big retailers named and shamed. Coles, IGA, Metcash, Coca-Cola. Keep a close eye on the weather. Really chilly this morning. Yell kids. Almost tropical compared to other temperatures around the state. What about minus 2.5 at Tuggeranong. Bowl Pal. Not a cloud in the sky. Nothing to keep the heat trapped. Big full moon. Good night for the snow resorts. Ten centimetres of the white stuff.

Feed the Man

Our butcher is a fine-boned specimen with a lightly tanned hide and silver hair. He knows his cuts. He knows to say in a gentle tone, 'Planning a slow cook?' in case you're under the impression chuck can be cooked in under an hour. I like to nod yes like a conspirator. When he's out the back with the carcasses I scan the metal trays inclined behind glass. Sauced kebabs, crumbed veal, small, netted woodland creatures, nestled in parsley. The shop is clean. Not a fingerprint, not a speck of blood in sight. To exit you press a large green button to shoosh open the door. It could be a spacecraft. Or a forensics lab – cold, clean, neat, housing bits of flesh, gristle, knives.

'Well, then'

Nothing stirred on the frosted fields. Ducks rose off the river silent as commas. Elizabeth pulled her coat tight. Cloudlets fluttered from her mouth as she bowed her head and traipsed on, catching sight as she did of her muddy hem. Just as the first low fingers of sun were extending their reach she looked up to see a figure approaching in an overcoat, unbuttoned. He strode towards her, not yet aware of her, shirt collar open at his chest.

'Mr Darcy!' she exclaimed.

'Miss Elizabeth,' he said, in surprise. 'What the fuck are you doing out at this ungodly hour? Only madmen and farmers up. It's freezing! Check out your shoes. You're soaked.'

'Yes, I suppose I am,' said Elizabeth, hoping, however, that her cheeks were flushed and her eyes fine.

'Your nose is as red as a cherry, mate. Best get home before you freeze solid. Like my nuts.' Darcy let out a loud laugh.

Elizabeth nodded, unsure where to look.

'Speaking of nuts,' he went on, flashing a large knife. 'Castration Day calls. Have a good one.'

Elizabeth moved aside to let Mr Darcy pass in his great boots. Her feet were indeed cold and wet. Time to return to the homestead to set the fire and boil water for tea. Her sisters and mother would soon be awake and clamouring.

Between Dark and Dawn

He came to the decision in the hour between dark and dawn, Cathy dreaming on the pillow beside him, slats of moonlight across her cheek.

In time Ben would understand. The boy was resilient, wild, independent. Forever running the length of the paddocks, along the fencelines. Climbing boulders to sing to the cloudless sky, flapping his arms like a fledgling eagle.

He had a notion Cathy expected it. She was hollow-eyed, hollow-necked. Watching him.

The farm had bowed them both. Starting out, they'd had no idea – bellies full of hope at the wide horizons, the nights of dazzling stars. The new baby.

He eased his legs out of bed. Cathy stirred, but didn't wake. In the bathroom he pulled on his jeans. Ran his fingers through his coarse hair. His face was an ashen outline in the mirror.

Into Ben's room now. His sleeping boy in shortie pyjamas – legs, arms awry, hair every which way. He leant down to kiss his forehead, then turned to go.

Daddy?

Sh. Go back to sleep.

Ben cycled the covers off and sat up. Daddy, he whispered, hopping down and padding over. I want to come with you.

He considered for the smallest moment, then said, Put on your jacket. And these pants. Sh, now. We can't wake Mummy.

How could he take the boy? he wondered. But at the same time, now that he was so close, how could he even think of leaving him behind?

Welcome Party

They marvelled at the gleaming platters – the side dishes of water, the pilchards, the sandy burrow stacked with beetles, the stale bread, slimy weed. Wandering Albatross had blundered in first, bewildered at yet another location. Pigeon, humble, apologetic – *just crumbs for me* – followed soon. Then Duck – brash, assertive, sporting a fancy emerald cravat. No one had noticed Mole's arrival, but all of a sudden there it was. Said not a word all evening. Spent most of its time under the sand. You could hear a faint munching.

Cooks' War

I was meeting my boyfriend's parents for the first time. Angela, the mum, was nowhere to be seen. Bob, the dad, was cooking pork caramelised with kecap manis, onions and brown sugar.

'Smells delicious,' I said.

Bob said, 'No recipe!' as a kid would say, 'No hands!' on a bike or a swing.

I felt the urge to congratulate him, so I clapped, saying, 'Well done you,' but my boyfriend warned me with his eyes. I thought maybe his dad didn't like praise. Or maybe not from his son's girlfriend who was wearing a purple hat. To change the tone I said, 'My dad can't cook to save his life' only I accidentally said *savour* his life.

Bob looked surprised, or maybe wounded. I corrected my blunder.

'This is how cam-cam-camelised pork *should* look!' It was Angela, clutching her phone. 'Is yours going to look like this, my sweet?' She swiped another photo into view. 'And this? You haven't a hope. My. Sweet.'

She tottered back down the corridor using the walls for support.

Bob, seemingly so mild-mannered, suddenly extracted his head from the steam to holler in the direction of his retreating wife. '*Fish-o!*' he roared. '*Fish-o!*'

What sort of family had I walked into? But it was too late for this. I had fallen in love.

Deterioration

Winter swung by with fierce precision: icy windows, aggressive draughts, splintered fingernails. We both tried to think 'heat' instead of turning it on.

The cat's coat had fluffed and plumped in readiness for the season. She found swatches of sunlight on the floor no human body could occupy – we who were not lithe, curling, adaptable. For the cat, winter was no discomfort.

Ten o'clock one morning on our third cup of tea from the same tea bag we found ourselves wordlessly watching her sleep. Then, for no reason at all, Nige stood up, shuffled across the rug in his ugg boots and toed her awake.

Vent

He opened his mouth to tell her he didn't love her, but instead what he said was, You look amazing in that outfit and what have you done to your *hair*! It's so shiny and full of body. And when she began to melt, the wax creeping lava-like across the floor, he was forced to hop clear of the flames, the popping bubbles. He thought, maybe I should snuff her out while she's burning brightly, but he was pain-averse and by then in any case her entire body had softened and drooped into a vast puddle of gratitude. He had no trouble clearing it.

Take Us to People

Anna knew the risks. The storm had swollen waterways and all advice was to stay indoors. But she needed to get to the hospital. Away from the house with its eerie candles. She needed the comfort of doctors.

Rain lanced the headlights. She cranked up the wipers, then reached behind and placed her hand on Lachlan's forehead. Hot and dry. 'It's okay, Lachie. We'll be there soon.'

At the edge of the causeway, Anna yanked on the handbrake. 'Lachie, we're going to go fast through the water and it might be loud, but we'll be on the other side in no time.'

'Okay.'

She gunned the accelerator. Water gushed up alongside. Lachlan was quiet. She couldn't risk turning to check on him.

'It's going to be alright,' she called. 'We're almost there.'

Halfway across, the car stopped. Water pounded the doors, splashed the windows. 'Come *on*,' she urged, turning the key. *Take us across. Take us to people who can tell us things.* The engine sputtered into life. The headlights illuminated the road ahead. *Come on.* The engine roared and the wheels gripped; all at once they were through.

Anna stopped the car and tapped the interior light to check on Lachlan. His eyes were wide and still. Black.

'Lachie?' She reached over. 'Lachie?' His skin was hot, but not burning.

'Mum?' he whispered.

'Yes?'

'Can we do that again?'

Frost

His throat tightens in the chill air. The thermos holds hot comfort. He is companionless, save for the white-eyed crow feather-plumping on a bare branch. His line whirs an arc over the still lake. A motorbike whines up the mountain road behind him. He's a long way from the city. From his child, just waking, stretching her bed-warm arms, padding bleary to the bathroom. In the kitchen now, a jam-smeared, knotty-haired chatterbox swinging her legs on *her* weekend/*his* weekend/*hers*/*his* – rotating loneliness *into*/*out of*/*into*. Heart. The water ripples, plops. His fingers cramp. The frost glitters.

Fact or Fiction?

'What does that mean, Gran? Turn the other cheek?'

Harriet's polishing cloth was like a crumpled brown flag, flapping eagerly. 'It means walk away from your aggressor. Never fight back. Do *not* react.'

Dominic caught a whiff of furniture wax that both nauseated and comforted. 'But Gran – he won't leave me alone no matter what.'

'Ignore him,' she commanded. 'In time he'll give up and move on.'

Dominic touched the bruise on his forearm. 'So, I should just let him twist my arm? Rub my face in the dirt?'

'This is what he does?' asked Harriet.

Dominic nodded his waterbird head and took a slight step to the right. 'And look at these.' He pointed to his calf muscle with its cluster of angry-looking blisters.

Harriet flung the cloth over her shoulder and took the Bible from the side table. 'I'm sure,' she said, thumbing through it, 'I'm sure that's what it says. It doesn't sound right,' she whispered. 'Not right at all. Could I have misinterpreted things? There must be another verse.'

Fracking

May sourced knitting needles and wool from craft shops, op shops and friends. On winter mornings she sat outside council chambers with all the other Knitting Nannas Against CSG. The moniker irritated, since May had never been a nanna, or indeed a mama. In 1949 the kitchen had borne witness to her labour and dead infant. Her husband had left to sire afresh. Over the years May's pile of knitted booties, caps, shawls and wraps discoloured, until one morning she woke and began to unpick, unravel, re-roll. She knitted for the new baby down the road. She knitted for Doris's pug. She knitted a tea cosy for dear old Rupert at the RSL. She knitted to save the planet, herself.

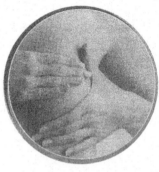

Broken down

Sliding his hand around the belly of the machine, the plumber extracted two mangled breast pads. *Guilty*, he said in triumph. I told him I'd hand-wash in future. In my arms was six-week-old Nathan who'd just woken. My breasts were tingling and I knew before long I'd spring a leak through my t-shirt. The plumber eased his stubby finger into the curl of Nathan's hand. *Hungry, is he?* I nodded. I stifled a yawn, but felt like crying. The plumber's business name – I can't remember it now, but his blue shirt bore a stitched-on label – Plumb the Depths? All Your Troubles Will Drain Away? A play on words that exposed a fresh wound in me, and all at once I felt like hurling myself at his chest and sobbing on his broad tradie shoulder. Instead I mumbled something about fetching my purse and scurried into the kitchen. I could hear him packing up his tools. I thought of offering him a coffee, but he'd already mentioned double-booking to squeeze me in. Forty dollars would do, he said, as I met him in the hall. I handed him cash, laying the notes on his broad, cushiony palm. *Don't give your mum any trouble*, the plumber said to Nathan, tweaking his little toes. I watched through the window as he climbed into his van. The sign on the side – I just can't remember it now.

esc

So now he only speaks keyboard: *shift* for move out of my way. If he doesn't like what I say (always): *delete*. When I go shopping he points to the clock on the wall: *return*. He uses *fn* instead of fucken – one saving grace.

When he's in the bathroom I study the keyboard. On the left, *option* is trapped between *control* and *command*. *Space* – between two *commands*. Then I see it. Up the top – in the corner – *esc*. Right on the edge. All I have to do is close the windows. Leap.

Booster

Skating down supermarket aisles, a rakish red hat on her head, would be a *positive* activity, Connie assured her shrink.

Angling her Golf into a Parents with Prams space, she sat for a moment, listening to the engine tick. On the seat beside her, the red hat and rollerblades seemed drained of positive. Terrifying, in fact. Illegal too? Nonetheless, one of the most useful pieces of shrink advice thus far was to *not back down*. To back down was defeatist, negative, and this was what Connie was attempting to move beyond.

A tap on her window. Face like a fried tomato. Babe in arms. *Are you a PARENT?* the woman screamed, searching the back seat with her eyes. Connie tried to focus. Was she?

Where's the kid? The woman's neck was all cords. Sunglasses atop her head like bat wings.

Connie shrugged, and opened her hands helplessly, trying to form words. She couldn't remember, couldn't remember. *Turn this into a positive.* The shrink's milk-honey voice in her ear: *Anything and everything can be turned into a positive. All it takes is self-belief: I can, I can, I am, I am.*

Drought

The kid calls, 'Hey. Got any spare change?'

    I toss him twenty cents.

    'What do I do with this?'

    I shrug. 'Save it for a rainy day.'

    'We ain't had rain in months.'

    I shrug again. 'Spend. Don't spend. It's nothing to me.'

    '*You're* nothing, you big fat loser.'

    'Loser? Give me back my money.'

    'No way.' The kid starts running.

    'But you said you couldn't use it,' I call after him.

    'Isn't that…' The kid laughs as he holds out his palm. 'Isn't that rain?'

Exhibition

The tall woman, the American, said she was over here to find a life partner. She was from the Midwest, she said. A long way to come for a life partner, I said. Don't they exist in the US? Oh, but my husband left me a couple of million, so I can afford it. So you've had one life partner already? His life, not mine, she quipped. She was good-looking, probably late forties, hard to tell. I nibbled on a doll-sized salmon quiche and said, So do you think exhibition launches attract life-partner types? But before she could answer, a silver fox sidled up to her with champagne. Congratulations on your work, the man said. Magnificent. Your best collection to date. Well, the smile that dazzled. She glowed like molten steel.

Inheritance

We lived on a farm for a while. A small one. Dad loved it but Mum couldn't stand the isolation and the heat. One day she just up and left. Came home from school to a note on my pillow. I was sixteen. She loved me but was dying inside, she said. Look after your dad, she said. So I tried but I had exams and no time to be cooking and cleaning. We fought terribly, my dad and me. One day I screamed I'm not your *wife*. He slapped me hard across the mouth so I packed my bag and my books and went to a friend's house. Her parents didn't know what to do with me, but when I twigged they were set to report me I hitched to the bus station and caught an overnighter to the city and this is where I am now. It's a squat, it's dry, and there are about six of us. I try to keep my nose clean but it's hard not to zone out sometimes. I wanted to be a vet. There goes that dream.

Whimbrel

The rarely sighted whimbrel. A seven-whistler ti-ti-ti-ti-ti-ti-ti. Evan up a tree with the bird book. Fond of birds, Evan. Small and noticeably paler. Coastal mudflat dweller. In adverse weather might overshoot during migration. Evan wants to shoot. Not a bird. The ostrich is a large flightless bird. Long, naked thighs, long, naked neck. Voice a loud, hollow booming. A guttural ratcheting. Evan wants to shoot heavy, flightless Addison. Addison with his flock of feral bullies. Evan can fly. Over islands, estuaries. Evan can fly.

Narcissus

Winter was mild that year. The lawn continued to push up thick blades by the thousands and she never seemed to wear anything heavier than cotton. On her walks along the beach, the water was kind to her feet and she often saw children playing bare-backed with buckets and spades. The only indication of the season was the early dark, making the evenings long and quiet.

After she'd fed the dog, watched the evening news, eaten or not eaten a scant meal, she'd sit in the lamplight, twisting her wedding band. She'd pick up a book, only to put it down again. She'd move to his chair and wriggle her bottom into its velvet crater. She'd lean into the wing's worn patch, where his head used to rest when he slept, his hair nudged up, glasses awry. Now and then he'd open his eyes and say, What's happening? to which she'd reply, All's well, or later, Fancy a warm milk? and then, handing it to him would be met with such a look of gratitude and love that she'd say, Oh stop it, you old thing. He'd wink and say, Bedtime yet?

The narcissus bloomed early that winter. She woke one morning pierced by its scent and decided not to get up. Not until she had to.

Loadbearing

George had been laying bricks for almost thirty years, and had taken on the complexion, even the texture and heft, of a brick. He found himself sinking to the bottom of the local pool, or hurled through windows. Once, while waiting on the station platform, he'd been tagged. The thought of retirement was like a welcome lamp to George, but his wife had other ideas. All he needed was *sloughing*, a new word she'd picked up at the parlour where she'd started a job – a career change, really – that was all about skin. But on the morning of his sloughing appointment George woke to find himself rendered from head to toe, which, although it was a clean, fresh look, had inundated his cells. Asphyxia was bound to follow.

Hardware

I'm directing my trolley hesitantly towards bathroom accessories when I hear a hello. I turn to see my ex and his partner.

Hello, I say, smiling pleasantly while inwardly saying *shit, of all places*. I blurt out, Where are the kids? and it sounds accusatory even though the kids are old enough to be left at home and I do it all the time.

Apparently one of them is still in bed.

Get him up! I let fly. It's a beautiful day. Almost midday!

My ex's partner looks at me and says condescendingly, It's all very well to tell him to get up, but if he doesn't want to...

Oh really? Please don't tell me about my son.

She's in her silly denim shorts, which, I'm sorry, are just wrong.

We get off the topic of the kids and onto why I'm in Bunnings. She says she never expected to see me here and I say I come here a lot, thinking *why would she think that?*

I launch into a list of things I'm fixing in my bathroom and when I realise I'm mainly talking directly to my ex about measurements and fittings and about the helpful bloke from the Grey Army I turn to include his partner because I'm nice like that.

She says, The Grey Army is great.

I nod.

As we part ways, I ask, What are you here for?

Screws, my ex says. Screws.

Manifesto for a Woman Walker

Send me west into the untamed night, free and without baggage. Send me light and head-clear, without covering but with solid shoes and dry socks, that I may hike the long byways, the fields, hills and riverbanks, that I may enter pubs for a meal and a beer, sleep wide and loose, the stars disinterested, dazzling little pockets that hold me until dawn when the dew, settled on my cheek, dries quickly in the sun.

outlet

he told his dad he was taking sally for a walk, it's a bit late isn't it? mumbled his dad, but he said nah, not really the streetlights are on anyway and his dad grunted into his beer and flicked the remote, so he didn't take sally but sprinted up the road not looking back until he came to the bush, the air was tinder hot and crackled his blood, above him the trees whispered in the barely breeze and in the distance a truck braked, the sticks under his feet split and cracked, he brushed past ferns, he knew the way, been up here often enough it was *his* place, only once had he seen anyone, an old lady bending over a flower with a magnifying glass, she'd jumped but then smiled and said hello, nice smile she had, gentle like his nan's, this was a good spot nice and cracker dry, within seconds his ball of paper was alight and then the twigs he'd set over it and then licks of, snakes of, lovely flame, and pops and cracks and explosions, soon he had to stand back from the heat and knew it was time to go but he couldn't stop watching and now fire tearing up a trunk and he really had to run so he scrambled, scrabbled down the trail and onto the road dodging lamplight, heart crowding his chest and back home his dad said sally been whining and whining didn't you take her? where you been? I smell smoke

Retreat

The cave had been beckoning all morning. The sign at the entrance warned of rock-falls but really it was an at-your-own-risk cave on this remote peninsula. Behind her the sand shone. Among the other holidaymakers were the twins and her husband, holding hands, making for the water. Kyle urging his father forward, *Quick, quick*, keen to plunge. Jasper pulling back, nervous of the waves. Kyle's eyes had flipped open at birth, little fists punching the air, defying the world with his bellow. Jasper's cries were plaintive, continuous, like a trapped mosquito. Just now he'd whined, *Mummy, don't go, don't go.* Cheerily she'd replied, *Just for a walk. Back soon.* Her eyes soon adapted to the gloom. The further in she went, the fainter grew the slosh of the shore waves. At the far end she found a narrow opening. She took out her torch, concealed beneath her shirt, climbed in and began to crawl, without looking back.

Illusion

The moon rests on a gum's withered limb. A mopoke hoots under cover of dark. A cat stalks a rodent, barely disturbing the grass. One light at a window. One hand at a blind. One smash of a glass. One yell. One whack. One cry of a child. The mopoke's wings are black flags, tipped with light. The moon has risen, grown smaller.

Values

The new kid in school, her name is Bec. I guess it's short for Rebecca. I like the name. My name can't be shortened. I have a one-syllable name. Bec's hair is wild. Bec's legs are long and wiry. She can run so fast. I like to run but I have to walk like a l-a-d-y. None of this barefoot malarkey, either. When Bec's out the school gate she whips off her shoes and socks and just *flies* home. I wish I knew where she lived. One day I'm going to follow her. Maybe I can give her some money and she'll take me to her house to play. My dad says everyone can be bought. Maybe I can buy Bec.

Mona Lisa

Where are her eyebrows?

    What? said Graham.

    Her eyebrows. She's hairless.

    I've never noticed.

    I stood on tiptoes for another glimpse. And it's *tiny*.

    But what do you think of *her*?

    I shrugged. What's all the fuss about?

    Graham frowned.

    No eyelashes either.

    Graham said, You're missing *le point*.

    Oh? What is *le point*?

    The mystery. The quiet. The smile that isn't always a smile.

    Well. Give me *Liberty* with her hairy pits leading the people any day.

    Graham's frown deepened. I can't believe your reaction. This is da Vinci, and one of the most exquisite—

Is this how you think *I* should be? Because I'm not. I'm not this.

Don't be ridiculous. It's a 500-year-old painting! Take a look at the crowds.

I know! I twirled my arms around. It's crazy if you ask me.

Sh. Keep your voice down.

Ooh. Am I being too loud? Too emotional? Are my eyebrows all ugly and screwed up?

Graham raised his eyes to the ornate ceiling.

Aux armes! I cried, fist aloft. If you want me I'll be at *Liberty* in Room 77.

Tough Love

The first thing her father said when he brought her home from hospital was, 'No concessions. Here, take this wooden spoon and go and make yourself a cup of tea.'

'What's the spoon for?' she asked.

'That's so you can reach the switch.'

Rescued

The well had dried up long ago, and was now a deep, dark hole that stank of old earth, bleeding teeth and rain. Amber remembered her mother emerging from the laundry with a small sack that bulged and rippled. Every spring the same thing. Afterwards, Amber would climb on the log to rest her chin on the well's cold stone lip. She would concentrate hard, listen. Hoping there would be no sound, and at the same time hoping there would. Often she heard the faintest noise – as she imagined a star would make, falling. She remembered this now, standing in front of the shop window, the cat's golden eyes looking back: pick me, pick me.

We Should So Try That

To spice things up they tried *Bachelor*-type dates. Oh, my god, you look incredible, stunning, they'd say to each other, before stepping into a limousine one of them had hired. Meanwhile, the other had arranged a speedboat to take them to a private performance – a Cossack dancer – and they'd gaze entranced at this and, later, at the champagne and sweetmeats. Despite her blistered heels and his collar rash, they continued to greet the small, tender compliments spilling from each other's lips with elegant appreciation. By nightfall they'd be exhausted; the crew would strike the lights and depart, leaving them on a faux-leather couch in a meadow, uncomfortable and cold.

Plumbing

Pete would rather a sweeter job. A confectionary seller, for instance, or a masseuse – scented almond oil, perfumed towels. Or a gardener – tending jasmine, gardenia, rose. Pete considered these options when elbow-deep in shit, when digging trenches, when brown pipe-water spritzed his face. But once home, showered, changed and preparing a pie and salad for himself and Kirsten, life seemed sweet again. After dinner, Kirsten's smooth arms would circle his neck; they'd watch a movie, make love. Nothing sweeter than this, he thought. It was only after midnight, his work gear glowering in the corner under the digital clock, a silent text blinking on Kirsten's phone, only then did Pete wonder.

Hold-up

Rain scuds the late-night servo. A van in a parking bay, bearded driver asleep. A car at a pump. In the shop, Mrs Mac's pies sit in the warming box. A man in a hoodie thumbs through girlie mags under the white light. As the car leaves the pump, he fronts the counter. The attendant's palms rise. Empty the till, says the hoodie, waving his pistol. Okay, says the attendant. It's not. Is it? Davo? Morton Primary? Shut up and give me the money. Okay, says the attendant. I remember now. Fish paste sandwiches. When I didn' bring me lunch, ya'd share. Ya had the best sandwiches. Meanwhile the van driver wakes, rakes his beard. Climbs down and heads for the glass doors. At the sight of the gun he backs off. Whattaya need it for, Davo? the attendant is saying. Ya hungry? I can give ya a pie. Take a pie, Davo. Go on. As the van driver pulls out his phone his hi-vis vest gleams. It catches the hoodie's eye.

What He Needs

He was drawn to Veronica's eyes like a moth to a sensor light. Flit away, flit back. Flick on, flick off. He felt no guilt. Mandy had been so moody since her father's death – not that he blamed her, and he'd certainly been a brilliant man and a devoted husband and father – but surely there comes a time when grief dissolves and you return to the land of the living? Every night she was in bed early and asleep when he got there, or pretending to be. Up at dawn and out the door for a run. Back and into the shower just as he was finishing his coffee. Clearly avoiding him. So who could blame him for falling for Veronica's eyes? Veronica. The name electrified him. Mandy rhymed with blandy. Nothing had happened. But the signs were there. The casual brush of an elbow. The sidelong glance. Catching the lift together. And her scent! Mandy's White Diamonds was beginning to sicken him. Her mother to dinner tonight. Dreading it. When was he planning to finish the deck? The carport? There'd be remarks on his drinking. As if he's falling about drunk! These bloody women boxing him in, stifling him. Veronica was different. Veronica would let him *be*. She was everything he needed.

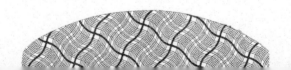

Rats

She balled the toilet tissue and stuffed it in the plughole. That should stop the rats. Outside the bathroom window an earnest conversation was taking place. … *marbles*, she heard. Huh, they think I've lost 'em. … *in a home*. She smacked her palm on the high frosted window. Don't think I can't hear you! *And* I can smell your cigarettes. Rats, rats, the lot of you. Nibbling away at me. Go home to your families. No one's pitching me out. She glanced in the mirror. Wild hair. Nightie unbuttoned. Who *was* that?

First Quarter

Cora gripped the brush in the glare of the art class lights. Rough, red, clumsy, her hands bore the legacy of her working life: bleach, furniture wax, polishing rags. Hot with embarrassment she daubed and streaked, willing form and grace onto the canvas. In time, the understanding that others in the class focused more on their art than her hands encouraged her. As did the comments from Gabriela whose breath, as she leaned in to observe, slid past Cora's bare shoulder. Her shapes grew more complex, the colours and lines more assured. She grew attentive to shadows and light. One evening in class Gabriela laid her hand between Cora's shoulder blades. Cora pulled away, her body darkening with shame even as it thrilled. She imagined her hands chafing the tutor's skin, the retreat. She stared at her palms where they lay inert on her lap, and flinched as Gabriela eased the brush from between her fingers. Gabriela proceeded to drag broad bands of moss green, then rust red, and cerulean across Cora's palms, until they were landscapes – rugged, forested, wild. Cora looked down, then with one sure movement made her mark on the canvas. That night she hugged her hands under her armpits and her skin was new, her bed a moon.

Broken Windows

Maestro raises his baton. The audience waits in anticipation for the crash of cymbals that will leave them shuddering. In the glow of the footlights the baton quivers. All eyes focus on its tip. Sweat drips off maestro's nose. A voice from the stalls cries *Wait!* The crowd titters, tsks, murmurs. Disgraceful child. Take it out. The orchestra members glance at each other, lower their bows. *Wait!* The child's voice is high, unbroken. One of schoolboys from St Angelis. A treat, an outing, a privilege to be at the performance. How *dare* he? Heads turn. Ushers descend and lean in towards the teacher in charge. Three things happen next: a boiled lolly flies in a high arc from the dress circle, a balled-up program hits the lead violinist in the head, and in the front row, a white-haired gentleman stands and brandishes his walking stick: *Oi, Maestro! Oi, Maestro!*

Anchor

Heat shimmered off the road. Even if her dad still lived in Brentwell Street he mightn't be home. He could have a job, hah-hah. Not once in ten years had he mentioned work. Ten years since he'd left, kicked off the steelworks for constantly turning up pissed. Kicked out by her mum. His phone-calls and letters, always muddled and rambling, grew less and less frequent. Until they stopped. She unfolded her grubby printout of a grid of streets. Brentwell was round the next corner. She walked along checking off each number until she stood outside a neat blue fibro. Beds of flowers flanked the steps. Heavy tomatoes adorned the sunny wall. And there it was: the brass anchor doorknocker, the one thing he'd taken with him. Her knock echoed hollowly. Yapping on the other side. Her heart lifted. He has a dog. If he could care for a pet... She knocked again. Not home. She sat on the top step and turned the printout over. She wrote about the baby. Due in five months, just before his birthday, she said. You're going to be a grandad. She'd be hitching back that afternoon. Your dog sounds cute. Here's my address in case you're ever passing. Later, back on the highway, a car pulled up. At the window a face – thinner, bearded, but those eyes, she'd know them anywhere. Clear as clear. A grin the size of a welcome bridge. Got a feed ready. In you hop.

Grand Designs

It's June. Money is tight. Two friends come to help. One plays around on the digger. One flings tiles off the roof. We don't have much. We need a table. A couple of chairs. Great buildings don't need to be excessive. By autumn we're exhausted and over budget. I'm pregnant with our third child. We move in with my husband's parents when the weather causes work to stop. We visit Father Christmas and the kids are terrified. He smells of brandy and you can see his undergarment. We buy pre-boxed gifts for everyone. I burn the pudding. Work starts again in February. Angela begins school. The teacher seems nice. *Why is she crying?* I can't answer. All we need is a table. A couple of bespoke chairs.

Flat Pact

Here on the porch I'd all but forgotten him, with the fragrance of jasmine, the green buds on the woody hibiscus, and the chuck-chuck of a wattlebird. 'Two minutes,' I whispered. 'I'm watching the sun set.'

His call grew insistent. 'Deirdre! You there?'

Of course I'm here. Day after day. Waiting on him hand and foot. This wasn't part of the deal. For better but not this worse. Nothing wrong with him really, he just can't seem to *get up*. Doc says on the quiet *depression or chronic fatigue*. Well, which is it? I want to yell at her. Scour your diagnostic encyclopaedias. Instead, I nod quietly and enfold my husband's hand in mine.

It was bound to happen. For forty years my love cells had played ignorant, and now pop, pop, pop – punctured like those tiny balloons in plastic wrap. Nothing left but a flat pack of detachment.

Burden

He tells me he raped a woman once. He tells me over coffee on a Sunday morning, as we share the morning papers, wait for our Eggs Benedict. We'd been married eight years. He looks relieved. But you know what? Now, that woman's burden is also mine. And it eats at me from that day on. Eats at me so much it pisses him off. So one day he brings his fist near my face and hisses *you're mine*, and I can see – *those* were the eyes, *that* was the voice he would have used.

The Present

The neighbourhood smells of mown lawns, mince pies and shortbread. Jacob is impatient for his mum to get home so they can go buy his dad a headlamp for camping. Trouble is Jacob hasn't been camping with his dad for a long time. Not Easter, not winter holidays and not yet this summer. He goes to a tennis camp, but it's not a real camp. All he does is walk to the courts every day and learn to hit and walk home again. Jacob wonders how his mum will react when he suggests the headlamp. Probably sigh with annoyance and shake her head. Maybe a card and a chocolate bar, Jacob. That's enough. You make the card.

Platitudes

It's like learning to drive, I say. Only there's no road. No car. No stop signs. Does that make sense? She nods, slowly. I rattle my car keys. Come on. All you have to do is put your foot on the pedal and go forward is what I mean. It's about going forward. Oh, yes, and you can't reverse. Ever. No looking in the rear-view mirror. So it's not *really* like driving a car, is it? she says, tying her laces. Okay, it's a clumsy metaphor, I say. Just that the idea is to go forward, not to regret things you've done or not done. My troubled daughter does not seem any less troubled. Anyway, I say, glancing at my watch, chocolate can be helpful too. Her mouth turns down. Just take the pressure off yourself. Enjoy life, I say. You're only young once. I'd give my eyeteeth. Time to go.

Catch-up

She scoped the tables. No sign of him. Good. Still time to go to the bathroom, reapply lipstick, buy a drink, steady herself. A whole *year*. Had she changed? Had he? She hadn't so much as glanced at anyone else, or if she had, it was only for comparison. No one had the Hollywood looks, the wit. The blond frizz on the back of the neck. Why had he called? Said he couldn't get her out of his mind. Said he'd made a mistake. She combed her hair, turned to look at the fit of her jeans in the mirror. At the bar she ordered a Riesling. Took a sip and chose a table in a quiet corner. The act of sitting alone – waiting – brought back memories. How many times? God. There he was. Peering in the window. Drop-dead. Still. She saw him take out his phone to answer a call. He was laughing, leaning into the building, brushing his fingers through his hair. The glow of the bar-sign falling across his cheek. Pocketing the phone now, adjusting his expression. She stood, drained her glass and headed for the door. Slipped past him before he recognised her.

First Love

'Fifty dollars!' said Katie. 'Who was it? Did you see? You're so lucky. Wow.'

She was so happy for him, thought Liam. He didn't have half her talent. As for the fifty – it was from the woman who wore smart dark suits and the same sky-blue scarf every day. He'd watch her stride along the tunnel and then almost imperceptibly slow down to listen to his playing as she passed.

Others would avert their eyes, check their phones, sneak a look in his hat. Maybe chuck in some coins. Kids giggled as they tossed in gumnuts and wrappers – never money. But the woman with the scarf... Once when he was playing a Bach piece he saw her hurry away and pull out a tissue.

Katie was talking. 'I made ten dollars today. Pretty good for a Wednesday. Putting it towards a new bow. You?'

Liam clicked his case shut. 'A bow's a good idea. Me, well –' he carefully slid the note into his wallet – 'where would you go to buy a woman's scarf?'

Misguided

I'm waiting for the concert to start when a yellow Labrador in a leather harness leads a young woman to the chair beside me. A security guard at an art gallery once motioned me away when I tried to pat a guide dog sitting alongside its owner. I was at a loss. Does patting momentarily *mis*guide the dog? This was not something I remembered being taught. I felt foolish and stared at. You make a blunder, suffer embarrassment and shame, and this stays with you for life.

I'm falling into the Labrador's eyes. The woman's hands are curled on her lap, quite still. I sneak a glance at her profile. The violins are flying headlong into Vivaldi's winter gale, normally enough to catapult me into a conducting frenzy. Her face is as blank as a pale lamp. I've always imagined music to affect the sight-impaired more intensely. Is it possible she feels nothing?

When there's a break in the program, she whispers, without moving her head, 'You can pat her, if you like. I don't mind.'

'Oh,' I say. 'I thought it wasn't allowed.' I reach across to ruffle the dog's ears. It smiles at me. Of this I am convinced.

When I turn to offer my thanks, I see a tear gliding ever so slowly down the woman's cheek.

Lights

Another red light. He palms his chin, taps the steering wheel. Sport-plus-shopping traffic. Next to him his wife is silent. What a way to spend Saturday morning, stuck in the car with her in a mood. His head hurts from last night. That's why she's pissed off. Green, but only two cars make it through. The hulking yellow and blue sign taunts in the distance. Bloody IKEA. He can't stand the place. Full of pregnant women nesting. Her mother coming from the UK and they have to set up Home Beautiful. Bed. Lamp. Side table. Even a rug. What's the point in her visiting now? She hasn't said a word since they left home. Neither will he. Play that game. Good at it. Coloured streamers on cars. Must be junior grand final. Rather be cheering on the sidelines instead of shopping. Makes a fist – small as this, he was. Small enough to fit in his hand. Their boy. Won't think about it. No one's fault. Don't think about it. Green. Slams on the accelerator. This time he'll make it through.

How Do We Do This?

The first thing I noticed on entering his bedroom was a collection of *Star Wars* figures lining a purpose-built shelf. The second was his patchwork quilt. The third was how much I wanted to leave. But I was tipsy and his hands had already removed my shirt. We fell heavily onto his bed. The dating website listed a host of precautions and I was ignoring them all. I'd even let him buy me a drink while I was in the club's bathroom. What I knew about him was nothing. After a few clumsy minutes I sat up. Darth Vader taunted my quaking knees. Princess Leia's gown screamed *cover yourself*. I said, I'm sorry, I can't do this, and immediately felt sorry for saying sorry. He should be sorry. We should both be sorry. How was this act supposed to relieve loneliness? As I braced myself for his reaction I couldn't resist a glance at his chest with its soft brush of grey hairs, and then my eyes were drawn to a spray of faded freckles over his breastbone. He buttoned up my shirt, put on his, followed by the kettle. His two-burner stove was clean as a whistle. On his tiny windowsill a vase of daisies. I was already thinking that during our brief fumble on the bed his sheets smelt good. His skin, too.

Acknowledgements

I am enormously grateful to Bronwyn Mehan, the brains and brilliance behind Spineless Wonders. Without Bronwyn's championing of microfiction, in the shape of the joanne burns Microlit Award, and publishing opportunities, this book may never have materialised.

To the creative and talented Bettina Kaiser, whose stunning cover and illustrations give *Loopholes* such a distinctive look – thank you. Thanks also to Annie Parkinson for her editorial insights, and to Shady Cosgrove for her gracious Foreword. To Nicole Schalchlin, lovely intern in charge of publicity, many thanks for such care and effort. A warm thankyou to Janet Hutchinson for her feedback on my first forays into the short form.

Finally, heartfelt thanks go to Thursday writers Linda Godfrey, Ali Jane Smith, Fay Ryan, Andrea Gawthorne and Elizabeth Hodgson for their candid critiques, humour and friendship, and for indulging my microfiction obsession. Thanks to Jill, aka Samantha, for her unstinting interest, and to Scotti and Alec, who keep my imagination humming.

The following stories have been previously published:

'Monoculus' – *Seizure* (Online) (October 2015)

'Safekeeping' – *Out of Place* (Spineless Wonders, 2015)

'Breakdown' – *Cuttlefish* (1, 2015)

'How Do We Do This?' – *Cuttlefish* (1, 2015)

'Hold-up' – *Flashing the Square* (Spineless Wonders, 2014)

'Lights' – *Flashing the Square* (Spineless Wonders, 2014)

'Spathiphyllum' – *The Mozzie* (ed. Ron Heard), 2007

'Between Dark and Dawn' was a finalist in the Peter Cowan Writers Centre 600-word Short Story Competition, 2016.

'Hold-up' won the 2014 joanne burns/Flashing the Square competition, and was flashed onscreen in Federation Square during the 2014 Melbourne Writers Festival.

'Manifesto for a Woman Walker' was prompted by an entry from the journal of Sylvia Plath.

The epigraph is by Charles Baudelaire, translated by Louise Varese, from *Paris Spleen*, copyright ©1947 by New Directions Publishing Corp. Reprinted by permission of New Directions Publishing Corp.

CPSIA information can be obtained
w.ICGtesting.com
in the USA
03s0958131216
48BV00008B/45/P